# TERRIBLE THINGS
## COULD HAPPEN

*story and pictures by* NED DELANEY

Lothrop, Lee & Shepard Books
New York

**Library of Congress Cataloging in Publication Data.** *Delaney, Ned. Terrible things could happen. Summary: Fired from the Crust and Flake Company in favor of the boss's nephew, a pie deliverer inadvertently turns defeat into victory. [1. Delivery of goods—Fiction. 2. Dogs—Fiction] I. Title. PZ7.D3732Te 1983 [E] 82-10051 ISBN 0-688-01282-5 ISBN 0-688-01284-1 (lib. bdg.)*

*For El Boogaloo*

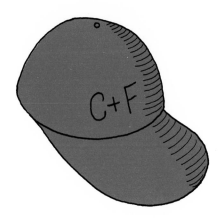

**W**aldo delivered pies for the Crust and Flake Company. He liked his job, and he was good at it too. He never dropped, bent, squashed, or, most important, sampled what he toted about town.

Waldo's boss at Crust and Flake was Mr. Grickle, who liked pies more than he liked Waldo. In fact, Mr. Grickle was secretly plotting to have Waldo fired. He wanted his nephew to have Waldo's job.

Bright and early one Monday morning, Waldo stepped into Mr. Grickle's office.

"Pay attention, Waldo," snarled Mr. Grickle. "Buster's Bistro wants ten Boiled Ant Pies by 3:46 this afternoon."

"I'm on my way," Waldo sang out.

"Snap to it," growled Mr. Grickle. "And remember, if you eat any pie, my nephew will have your job."

Waldo walked for hours, not stopping even for lunch. By the time he paused at the corner of Vinagaroon and Tulip Streets, he ached all over. He peered down Vinagaroon. Then, whistling nervously, Waldo stepped into the shadows.

Under the streetlight, five burly characters were planting roses. Waldo could only think of the terrible things that would happen if they got his pies. "Only crumbs will be left," he thought, "and I'll be the dessert."

He inched past the grisly gardeners, then, sighing with relief, he raced across the street and tripped on the curb. Ten pies sailed into the air. Waldo closed his eyes.

He felt something tap softly on his back again and again and again. It was Buster, grinning widely.

"Good show, old chap," said the bistro owner. "And precisely on time. Bravo."

10

Bright and early the next day, Waldo stepped into Mr. Grickle's office.

"What happened to your uniform, Waldo?" Mr. Grickle asked.

"Muggers were..." Waldo began.

"No excuses, Waldo!" interrupted Mr. Grickle. "By the way, do I smell Boiled Ant Pie on your breath?"

"Oh, no," replied Waldo. "That's the fried broccoli that I had for breakfast."

"Well," snapped Mr. Grickle, "Roscoe's Restaurant in Crunchville wants twenty-five Marinated Mud Pies not a second later than noon."

Waldo rushed to the airport and boarded the La Foote Twins' tiny plane. As it roared down the runway, Waldo gripped his tail.

"Please don't fly too high," he shouted, "it's my first airplane ride."

"Look at all the ants," exclaimed Waldo.

"Those aren't ants," said the co-pilot.

"Those are Crunchvillians," explained the pilot.

Waldo clamped his paws over his eyes, thinking of all the terrible things that were about to happen.

"A very big thunderstorm is just ahead," warned the co-pilot.

"Passengers will fasten their seatbelts," advised the pilot.

"Not me!" Waldo hollered, bailing out.

Dangling in the air, Waldo heard squawking and flapping. He felt a feathered grip on his paw. Waldo opened one eye. There was Roscoe, smiling broadly.

"Now that's what I call real pie delivery service," said the restaurant owner. "I'll double my order next week."

Bright and early Wednesday morning, Waldo stepped into Mr. Grickle's office.

"Do I see Marinated Mud Pie dribbling through your bandages, Waldo?" Mr. Grickle asked.

"Oh, no," Waldo hiccuped. "That's the squished squid I had for breakfast..."

"I've no time to quarrel," interrupted Mr. Grickle. "Lucy's Luncheonette across the bay needs fifty Clam Foo Young Pies by six o'clock sharp."

Waldo lugged the fifty pies down to the harbor and gingerly inched them aboard the Good Ship Dingle.

"Heave to and cast off starboard," commanded the skipper.

Soon Waldo tasted his squished squid again.

"I feel queasy," he told the skipper. "Is there a different route?"

"Aye, aye," nodded the Old Salt.

But instead of becoming calmer, the sea grew rougher. A wave splashed onto the deck of the ship and washed Waldo and his pies overboard.

Waldo paddled about, swallowing seawater. He felt seasick again, and this reminded him of Mr. Grickle and of all the terrible things that he would do when he learned of the waterlogged pies. Waldo was sinking fast when something floated up to him. It was the life preserver the skipper had thrown after him. Waldo squirmed inside the tube and stroked after his pies.

Toward sunset, he spotted land and his missing wares. They were drifting by bathers at the beach. Waldo groaned and closed his eyes just as a wave crested and sent him crashing onto the sand.

He bumped into a pair of feet. They belonged to Lucy, the owner of the luncheonette.

"A simply marvelous pie delivery," she said. "Absolutely perfect for our Flamingo Fandango."

As appreciation, Lucy fixed Waldo squished squid for dinner. He poured it into his hat.

Bright and early Thursday morning, Waldo stepped into Mr. Grickle's office.

"Is that Clam Foo Young Pie crust there under your kelp, Waldo?" asked Mr. Grickle suspiciously.

"Oh, no," answered Waldo. "They're only crumbs from the beet and garlic sandwich I had for breakfast."

"Not another silly story, Waldo," interrupted Mr. Grickle. "Bertha's Beanery needs ninety Stuffed Mosquito Pies in one hour. Hop to it."

"Bertha's Beanery is right next door," thought Waldo. "This delivery should be easy as pie."

When the ninetieth pie was stacked in place, Waldo pushed the heavy cart through the iron gate and onto the busy street. Suddenly

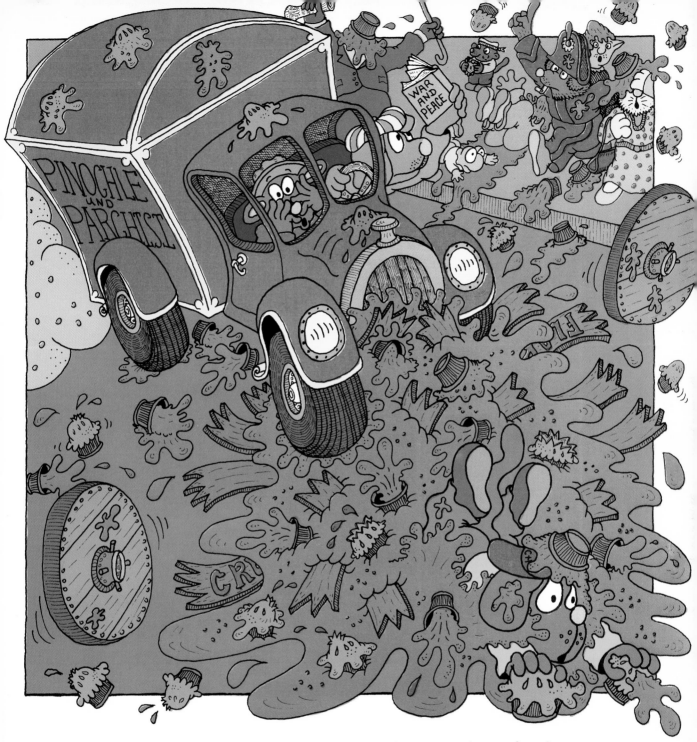

there was a loud screeching of tires. Waldo jumped to safety just as a truck careened into his cart.

"My pies..." moaned Waldo. "Maybe Bertha will like Squashed Stuffed Mosquito Pie instead."

Late that afternoon, Waldo walked slowly into Mr. Grickle's office.

"Bertha called to say that not one pie had reached her door," Mr. Grickle howled.

"Listen," pleaded Waldo. "Terrible things have been happening to me..."

"Do not lie, Waldo," interrupted Mr. Grickle. "You're covered with pie. I've finally caught you eating the goods. Now my nephew has your job."

"Oh dear," sighed Waldo. He didn't need to think about the terrible things that would happen. They just had.

For the rest of the day, Waldo sat sadly on the steps of Crust and Flake. He was still there at midnight, listening to the Night Watchman snore. Waldo was too unhappy to notice two sinister shadows pad stealthily past him. He was too dejected to see these masked figures pick the lock of the big oak door. Nor did the Night Watchman stir when the door to Mr. Grickle's office creaked open and the two culprits slipped inside.

The dastardly duo headed straight for the safe behind the oil painting of Mr. Flake. Much to the crooks' surprise, the safe was unlocked. A gleeful Mr. Grickle had forgotten to secure the door in his rush to celebrate Waldo's firing.

Suddenly Waldo remembered he had left his cap in Mr. Grickle's office. He decided to go get it then so he wouldn't have to face his old boss. He sneaked through the halls and tiptoed past the Night Watchman. Outside the office door, the smell of fresh pie wafted up from the ovens. Waldo remembered how much he liked his job. And how much he disliked Mr. Grickle. He began to growl. It made him feel much better, so he growled louder. Baring his teeth, he leaped into Mr. Grickle's office, thinking mean thoughts.

Hearing Waldo, the two robbers dropped the money and stuck their paws into the air.

"We surrender!" they shrieked.

Surprised, Waldo turned around to see who else was in the room and tripped on a cord, accidentally setting off the burglar alarm. The Night Watchman raced in. As he led the two desperadoes away, he told Waldo, "You've captured the thieves and saved the company payroll, the employees' retirement fund, and the homeless orphan donation. You'll be rewarded for this."

Bright and early Friday morning, the Crust and Flake Company thanked Waldo for his bravery. Mr. Flake told Waldo he would have free pies to eat for the rest of his life. Waldo politely asked for a portrait of a pie painted by a famous artist instead. Mr. Crust, who was retiring to Florida, named Waldo president of the company. Mr. Grickle's nephew was given his uncle's job. Mr. Grickle became pie deliverer. Business boomed and a statue of Waldo was erected in the town square.

Every morning on his way to the presidential chamber, Waldo would hear the nephew command, "Snap to it, Grickle. And remember, if you eat any pie, my cousin will have your job!"

Waldo couldn't help but chuckle.

NED DELANEY was born in Glenridge, New Jersey, the oldest of five children. "I've always had a wild imagination," he writes, "which caused endless trouble for me as a kid but is very useful to me now." Mr. Delaney attended the Art Institute of Boston, The Boston Museum School, and Tufts University, from which he received his B.F.A. A full-time writer and illustrator, he is perhaps best known for his picture books *Bert and Barney* and *Rufus the Doofus*. *Terrible Things Could Happen* is his first book for Lothrop. Mr. Delaney and his Newfoundland, Gatsby, live in a town near Boston that, he notes, "has the dubious distinction of being the birthplace of the fried clam."